ANIMAL ANTICS A TO Z

Sammy Skunk's Super Sniffer

by Barbara deRubertis • illustrated by R.W. Alley

THE KANE PRESS / NEW YORK

Alpha Betty's Class

Alexander Anteater

Bobby Baboon

Corky Cub

Dilly Dog

Eddie Elephant

Frances Frog

Gertie Gorilla

Hanna Hippo

Lana Llama

Izzy Impala

Jeremy Jackrabbit

Kylie Kangaroo

Maxwell Moose

Library of Congress Cataloging-in-Publication Data

deRubertis, Barbara.
Sammy Skunk's super sniffer / by Barbara deRubertis ; illustrated by R.W. Alley.
p. cm. — (Animal antics A to Z)
Summary: Sammy Skunk uses his amazing sense of smell and his cooking skills
to help the new school cook.
ISBN 978-1-57565-352-5 (library binding : alk. paper) — ISBN 978-1-57565-344-0
(pbk. : alk. paper) — ISBN 978-1-57565-383-9 (e-book)
[1. Smell—Fiction. 2. Senses and sensation—Fiction. 3. Skunks—Fiction. 4. Animals—Fiction.
5. Alphabet. 6. Humorous stories.] I. Alley, R. W. (Robert W.) ill. II. Title.
PZ7.D4475Sam 2011
[E]—dc22   2010051307

1 3 5 7 9 10 8 6 4 2

First published in the United States of America in 2011 by Kane Press, Inc.
Printed in the United States of America
WOZ0711

Series Editor: Juliana Hanford
Book Design: Edward Miller

Animal Antics A to Z is a registered trademark of Kane Press, Inc.

www.kanepress.com

Even when Sammy Skunk was just a little stinker, he had a super sniffer.

He liked to help his parents cook squash soup.
Sammy would sit on Papa's shoulders.
And Papa would stir the simmering soup.

"Sam, my man! What do you think?"
Papa would say.

Sammy would sniff. And sniff.

Sometimes Sammy smiled.
Mama and Papa knew what that meant.
The soup was good!

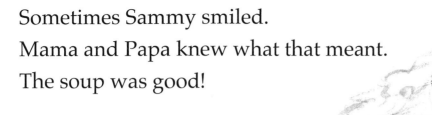

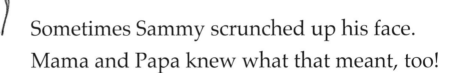

Sometimes Sammy scrunched up his face.
Mama and Papa knew what that meant, too!

"Oh, Sammykins!" Mama would say.
"What does the soup need?"
Then Sammy would point to something.
And Mama would sprinkle it in the pot.

Soon Sammy was an honest-to-goodness
soup expert!

Before Sammy started school, his parents told his teacher all about his super sniffer.

"How useful!" said his teacher, Alpha Betty.

At recess on the first day, Sammy put
his sniffer to work.
"Don't step there!" he called out.
And he pointed to some inky, stinky mud.

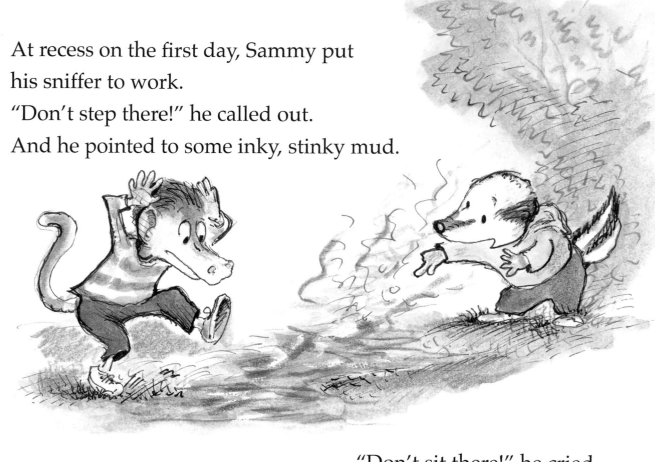

"Don't sit there!" he cried.
And he pointed to some icky,
sticky sap.

But when it was time for lunch, Sammy's
super sniffer caused a problem!

Alpha Betty led her class to the lunch room.
"Students, I'd like you to meet Susie Horse.
Susie is our new school cook.
She'll be fixing tasty soups for our lunches."

Susie served bowls of soup to everyone.

Sammy sniffed his soup.

He squinted his eyes.

He scrunched up his nose.

And he whispered, "Don't eat the soup!"

Susie Horse was NOT pleased.

"Is there a *problem* with my soup?"
she asked Sammy.

"I'm sorry, Susie," Sammy said.
He took a small sip of his soup.
Then he set down his spoon.
"I guess I'm just not hungry," he said.

No one else seemed hungry either.
Susie scowled.

The next day Susie served a different soup.
All the students watched Sammy.

He sniffed.
He squinted his eyes.
He scrunched up his nose.
And he tried to swallow a BIG spoonful of soup.

Suddenly Sammy *SNEEZED! A-SHOO!*

Soup spurted out of his mouth and his nose!

"I'm SO sorry, Susie," said Sammy.
He wiped up the soupy mess.
Susie was silent as a stone.
And her face was stormy!

Alpha Betty tried to explain about Sammy's sniffer.
Susie Horse still scowled. "Then let Mr. Super
Sniffer fix the soup," she said.

Alpha Betty smiled.
"Would you like to try, Sammy?" she asked.

"Sure," said Sammy. "If it's okay with Susie."

Susie's face still looked stormy.
"Okay, Mr. Super Sniffer," she said.
"Come back tomorrow morning during recess."

When Alpha Betty took Sammy to the kitchen
the next morning, he was shaking in his boots.

Susie's face was stormier than ever.

"Here's today's soup," Susie said.
She pointed to a steaming pot.

"What kind of soup is it?" Sammy asked.

"It's squash soup," said Susie.
"It's made with squash. And water."

"Oh!" said Sammy. "Sometimes I help my
parents make squash soup!
We add lots of stuff to make it super tasty."

Susie squinted her eyes.
"What sort of 'stuff'?" she asked.

"I'll show you!" said Sammy.
He scooped up carrots. Celery.
Onions. And apples!

Susie fussed as she sliced and diced.
"Apples in squash soup?
I've never heard of such a thing."

But Sammy was just getting started.

He said, "Shake in some of this and that.
Sprinkle in some of these and those.
Now smush it all together!"

Susie scowled as she smushed.
"This isn't squash soup," she snapped.
"This is a big, sloppy MESS."

Sammy took a looong, slooow sniff.
And he smiled a BIG smile.
"Taste it, Susie!" said Sammy.

Susie looked disgusted.
But she took a tiny sip.

She didn't smile.
But she didn't scowl either.

Then she slurped up a large spoonful.
The corners of her mouth twitched.
And slowly, Susie smiled a tiny little smile.

"Morning recess is over, Susie," said Sammy.
"I'll see you at lunch!"

Susie stared. Then she whispered,
"Thanks, Sammy."

At lunch, Susie served big bowls of squash soup.

Everyone's eyes were on Sammy.
He sniffed. He tasted.
And he smiled a BIG smile.

Today *everyone* was hungry!
No one talked. The only sound in the
lunch room was *slurping*!

Alpha Betty whispered in Susie's ear.
"The soup is simply delicious!"

Susie sat down next to Sammy Skunk.
"Will you bring your super sniffer to help
me tomorrow, Sammy?" she asked.

"Sure!" said Sammy.

And Susie smiled her BIGGEST smile.

Then everyone had a second helping of the best squash soup EVER!

Even Susie Horse!

STAR OF THE BOOK: THE SKUNK

FUN FACTS

- **Home:** Skunks live in North and South America and on some islands in Asia. They can dig their own holes for shelter . . . or live in hollow logs, rock piles, or even junk piles.
- **Appearance:** All skunks are striped, but there are many different patterns of stripes. Some skunks even have spots!
- **Food:** Skunks eat many different plants, insects, and small animals. They are also attracted to humans' garbage!
- **Did You Know?** Of course, skunks are best known for the VERY stinky liquid they spray when they are in danger. But *part* of this liquid has been used in making perfume!

LOOK BACK

Learning to identify letter sounds (phonemes) at the beginning, middle, and end of words is called "phonemic awareness."

- The word *soup* <u>starts</u> with the *s* sound. Listen to the words on page 22 being read again. When you hear a word that <u>starts</u> with the *s* sound, stand up and say "_____ starts with *sss*!"
- The word *mess* <u>ends</u> with the *s* sound. Listen to the words on page 11 being read again. When you hear a word that <u>ends</u> with the *s* sound, stand up and say "_____ ends with *sss*!"
- **Challenge:** The word *last* begins with the *l* sound and ends with the *s-t* sounds. Change the *l* to *f* and make a word that rhymes with *last*. Now change the *f* to *p* and make another word that rhymes with *last*.

TRY THIS!

Stand up and listen carefully as each word in the word bank below is read aloud slowly.

- If the word <u>begins</u> with the *s* sound, put your hands on your head!
- If the word has the *s* sound in the <u>middle</u>, put your hands on your tummy!
- If the word <u>ends</u> with the *s* sound, put your hands on your feet!

> skunk horse castle soup whisper
> hips useful sneeze guess sniff mess
> tasty stir boots fussing smile

FOR MORE ACTIVITIES, go to Sammy Skunk's website: www.kanepress.com/AnimalAntics/SammySkunk.html
You'll also find a recipe for Sammy Skunk's Squash Soup!